The Golden Snowflake

What Would You Wish For?

J.E. Wickert

It was a very, very cold winter's day.

And white snow fell from clouds of grey.

"Oh look," said grandfather. "Up in the sky!

I thought I saw it, oh my, oh my!"

"Saw what, grandfather?" the little boy said, Looking up at the sky by tilting his head.

"Do you mean the snowflakes so big falling down?

So thick and so fast that snow covers the ground?"

Grandfather then stopped and lowered his eyes, As he shook his head with whispered sighs.

"I thought for a moment..? But then it was gone.

All through the years I've been looking so long."

"What's gone, grandfather?" the little boy asked.

"What was it that's gone, what was it that passed?

When I look in the sky I see white flakes of snow.

Please tell me grandfather I do want to know."

Grandfather looked sad, but then said with a smile, "I've been looking and looking for such a long while.

I first started looking much younger than you, I might never see it, but I hope that you do."

"What is it, grandfather? I'll look for it too.

Just tell me grandfather I want to help you.

Is it something that only the winter will bring?

If it is we'll keep looking until it is spring?"

Grandfather smiled and lowered his head.

"I first learned about it in a book I read.

A very old book that's been lost in time
A very old book that was written in rhyme.

It's about something magic, so precious and true. But the story is known to only a few. Please keep it a secret for a secrets sake. It's the story about a Golden Snowflake."

"A Golden Snowflake?" the question was shouted.

And Grandfather knew that his story was doubted.

"I've not lied before, and I won't lie today,"

Grandfather then said, "So believe what I say.

"On a very special cold winter's day,

Perhaps one in a million no one can say.

A Golden Snowflake will come fluttering down In the billions of snowflakes that fall toward the ground.

To the one who can see it good fortune will come One only means one, one doesn't mean some.

Only one will be blessed to see such a sight.

Then he or she wishes with all of their might.

And whatever they wish for will surely come true, It's The Golden Snowflake's magic gift to you.

The Golden Snowflake will twinkle and shine, And nothing you've seen will have looked so fine.

It will glitter and glow just like any gold, And, if you could catch it, it wouldn't feel cold.

But in the old story I read in the book, No one can catch it—they only can look.

You must make your wish in it's twinkling light, Or your wish won't come true if it goes out of sight.

Do not try to catch it, it cannot be done.

It drifts farther away the faster you run."

"Where does it come from and where does it go?

Why can't we see it in each falling snow?

The grandfather's grandson looked up with wide eyes, And begged his grandfather with many more tries.

"I wish I could tell you, I wish that I knew."

The grandfather said, "But this I'll tell you.

No one can say—because nobody knows,

The secrets that fall in all winter snows.

"Once in a lifetime a gold snowflake will fall, Meant for one boy or girl, not meant for all.

The kinder the heart, the more chances they'll see, The Golden Snowflake meant for one he or she.

Only the good and the loyal and true—

And that's not the many, but only the few, Might be given the gift of the Golden Snowflake, And the one wish it offers the seer to make."

The little boy watched the white snow falling down, And turned this way and that as he looked all around.

But all he could see were snowflakes of white, As he squinted his eyes with all of his might.

"Let's go find it grandfather." the little boy said.

"Perhaps it is close and we'll see it ahead?

You look to the left and I'll look to the right I'm sure we will see its gold twinkling light."

Grandfather stood still—slowly shaking his head, "Let me tell you some more from the book that I read. Don't look for the Snowflake—that's not what to do. It's The Golden Snowflake that must come and find you.

You must always be good and be helpful and kind.

You must always keep love in your heart and your mind.

The Golden Snowflake will know if it's true, And that's when it might give it's gift to you."

"I have so many wishes I would like to make.

If only I could see the Golden Snowflake.

Why," asked the grandson, "does it give only one?

Why can't I wish and wish till I am done?"

A calmness came into old grandfather's voice.

"What's better to have—none—or only one choice?

But the one wish it gives and allows you to make, Shouldn't be for yourself, but for some others sake.

The Golden Snowflake keeps a secret so well, That only one wish should you ever tell.

If you wish for the happiness of a good friend, That happiness comes back to you in the end.

If you wish for peace and never for war, One wish is enough—you'll never need more.

If you do ever see The Golden Snowflake, Do you now understand the wish you should make?"

"I do, grandfather." was said with a smile.

"Lets go back home and get warm for awhile.

I will be good—and someday I might see, The Golden Snowflake falling down to me...

CPSIA information can be obtained at www.ICGtesting.com
Printed in the USA
BVIW12n0806300617
488221BV00008B/175